Annie Hoot
and the
Knitting Extravaganza

Holly Clifton-Brown

ANDERSEN PRESS

Annie Hoot was a kind but scatty little owl. She lived in a tree house deep in the woods.

She was always coming up with new ideas for things to do, and her latest craze was knitting.

She knitted morning, noon and night. She knitted jumpers, socks, hats and scarves.

She knitted squares, and stripes, and spots and stars. In fact, she knitted just about anything you could think of!

Sadly the
other owls
wouldn't wear the
clothes that Annie had
knitted for them.
"They are too bright," they said.
"We don't want to look different from
the other owls."
Annie decided to find some
animals who would want
her wonderful
woollies.
She knitted
herself a . . .

hot air balloon,

and off she sailed.

The wind blew her all the way to . . .

the rainforest.

It was a bit too wet for Annie's liking, but the treetops were full of the most exquisite birds she had ever seen.

"Don't worry," she told them. "I'll soon knit you something to keep you dry."

The birds were delighted, but as the rain continued to pour down, the knitted umbrellas began to sag. "We know who would really love your knitting, Annie," the birds said.

"The animals on the African plains get chilly at night." So Annie knitted herself a . . .

sail for a little wooden boat, and
she sailed across the sea.

She trekked up and down the dunes, and at last she arrived at the plains.

"I've come to knit you some lovely warm clothes to keep you snug at night," she told the animals.

She knitted long, stripy scarves for the giraffes, an enormous, jazzy jumper for the elephant and a huge hat for the big cat. But when the sun came up, the animals found the clothes too hot.

"Our friends at the north pole would love your knitting, Annie. It's cold all the time there," they said. So Annie knitted herself a . . .

parachute and glided over the mountains.

She skidded over

the icebergs and . . .

bumped into a polar bear's shivering bottom.

The arctic animals huddled round.
"I've come to knit you wonderful and warm things,"
Annie explained to them.

She knitted polka dot pullovers for the penguins,
a pair of dazzling diamond-patterned pyjamas for
the polar bear and a wonderful woolly
waistcoat for the walrus!

"Thank you, Annie. What cosy and colourful gifts!" they said. "Now we will be snug all the time!"

Annie was pleased that at last she had found some animals who really needed her knitting.

But she had run out of wool and she missed her tree house and the other owls, so she decided to fly all the way home.

"Hoot, hoot, hooray!

Annie's home!" the owls cried.

"We missed you so much, Annie, that we started wearing your wonderful woollies."

Annie was happy to be home and delighted to know her friends now loved her gifts.

" Annie, Annie," they cried.

"Please teach us to knit too."

And so Annie did.

And that very afternoon as they all knitted happily together, she told them about her travels and the amazing animals that she had met all round the world.

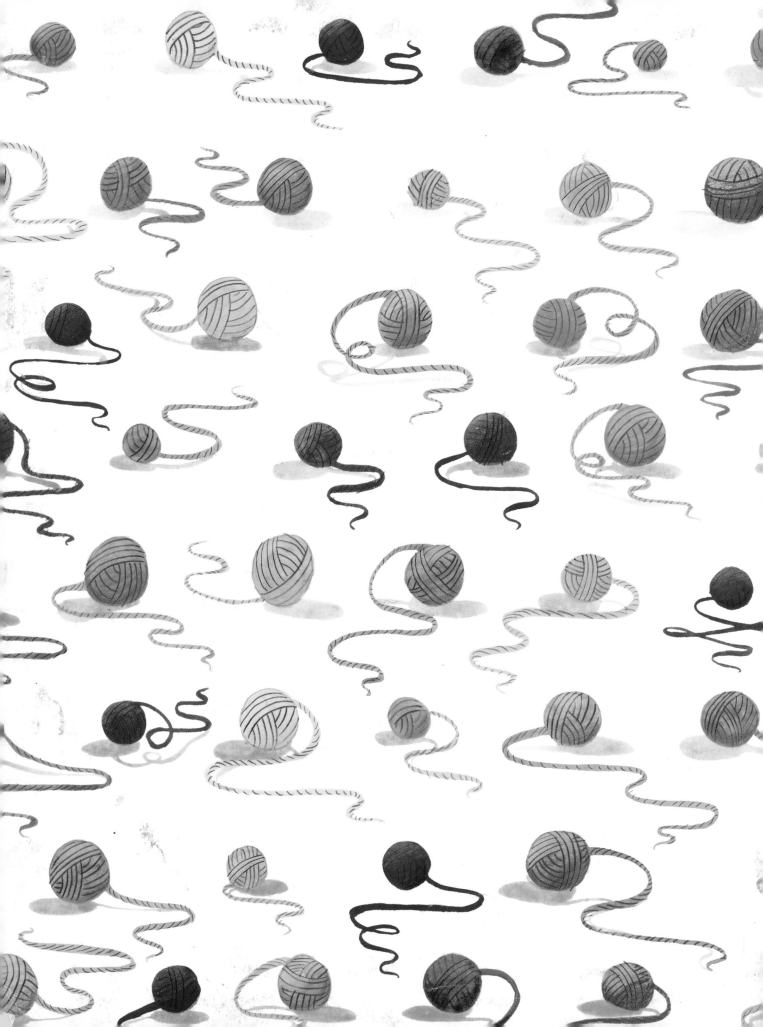